CHAPTER ONE

As I had scrubbed the grease from the pan I stared at Sheriff Randall walk towards the bar at a high speed. It was probably another country club fight as usual. Men get drunk and have a quarrel amongst each other over women that weren't theirs or perhaps knocking over their drink that they had spent their last nickel on.

Sheryl cry had captured my attention.

"What seems to be the problem?" I asked.

"Mr. Flake is acting crazy!" Sheryl replied. "I tried to stop him but he wouldn't listen."

"Where is he?"

"Out in the meadow. Next to the creek."

I glanced at the time knowing that Mrs.Rockmore would be arriving here shortly. But neither did I want to lose a horse. Especially one of the ones that I had received cuts and bruises to break them in.

"Stay here!" I said. "If Mrs.Rockmore arrives tell her I'll be back shortly."

CHAPTER TWO

While James removed the rotten wooden shelf Mrs. Pickett had stepped inside.

"Mr. Pickett!" James smiled. "What a pleasant surprise to see you. What brings you out this way."

"I was out by the creek and had seen your horse grazing out yonder!" Mr. Pickett replied. "Did you hear about them Buchannon boys?"

James continued to hammer the nails in place. He knew that those Buchannon boys were up to no good and was always causing mischief throughout the land that they came galloping through.

James broke the silence.

"Not since you have brought it to my attention." James said. "What are they a' doing now"

"Gunplay was spotted with that Micheals boy the other day." Mr. Pickett stated.

"Old Yellow?"

Mr. Pickett spit inside of the molten can that was laying over in the corner.

"Whatever that you want to call him." Mr. Pickett said. "That boys a wrecking ball by himself. Than those Buchannon boys right along with him aint a' looking too good." he added " What do you think we oughta do?"

James squenched his face.

"Lets not run around like ants in our pants." James said. "We don't want to start spreading any rumors, you hear me."

"But-"

"Give it some time. There's no telling what they might be up to." James added. "If things get out of hand then we'll give them a good fix."

CHAPTER THREE

When Gunplay had arrived at the small cave Old Yellow was fixing his saddle.

"I just went to town to check out things," Gunplay stated.

"Any signs of that ole' ranger." Old Yellow asked.

Gunplay shook his head in a noward motion.

"I didn't see him anywhere," Gunplay said. "I had stumbled across a few of his men though." Gunplay added tying down his horse. "Where are you headed?"

"Down by the creek. My canteen is a little dry as pine"

As Old Yellow rode off Gunslanger and Gunpowder came galloping up the hill.

"How's everything looking on your end?" Gunplay asked.

"There were a few cattle passing through," Gunpowder replied. "They should have cleared the place by tomorrow."

Gunplay sniffed heavily while fixing his britches.

"When are you thinking about making a move"

"When the rooster drinks some wine and the crickets starts to shine"

CHAPTER FOUR

The sound of a rattlesnakes rattler rattled as Gunplay had carried the wooden crates inside of the cave.

"How's things looking?" Gunplay asked.

Gunpowder removed the sweat that had spilled down his face.

"Probably a few more days at the most" Gunpowder replied. "It feels as if I'm digging in Plymouth Rock. Where's Old Yellow?"

"He went to town to grab a few things," Gunplay added. He tossed the crate into the corner making it more visible to the light."

"Any update on James."

"James and his boys have been sniffing up a storm around the place." Gunplay said. "We need to try to stay low and move cautiously"

"I hate them boys with a passion." Gunslanger mentioned. "I'll be glad when that day comes when I get a chance to sink a bullet in him."

Gunpowder blew snot from his nose. He heard sounds of hoofs striking the ground sensing that someone was about to approach them.

"Seems like we may have a little company a' coming our way," Gunpowder said. "You might a' want to go and check it out."

When Gunplay had made it to the entrance of the cave he stared down, noticing that it was some Indians approaching them.

"We have some Redskins moving in on us" Gunplay stated.

Gunplay removed his western smith while taking cover behind the huge rock that sat at the entrance of the cave.

BOOM. BOOM

"Get the horses," Gunplay added. He took another shot at the lead rider causing the horse to rear up. "There's no telling how many are trailing behind them. Let's get the hell out of here."

BOOM. BOOM.

CHAPTER FIVE

The sun was shining. The humidity was dry. I sat inside of the barn getting fresh milk pondering about when I was younger.
Whiskey husky voice barks interrupted my thoughts.

"If it ain't Kissing Kate" Wilbert smiled. "It had been a while since you and I had last talked."

I was surprised to see that it was Wilbert, a friend of mine that had taught me how to tie a decent knot.

"Where have you been hiding?" I asked.

"With all of this traveling from town to town. I could barely keep up with my own boot prints. How has things been going for you"

I sighed.

"The same I guess." I replied. "Keeping an out on Mrs. Rockmore."

"That's good to hear." he nodded. "How's Sheryl?"

"She's learning how to ride on her own"

"Hows shes coming"

"She's alright I guess"

Wilbert grabbed the kettle carrying it inside.

"Henry is catching on mighty fine" he said. "Sometimes he has me twirling on my heels."

Both laughed.

As Wilbert and I had shared with each other about the years that we had spent apart I noticed that it was getting late. I still had to drop off a few things throughout town before heading over to Mrs. Rockmore.
I aroused from the table cherishing the little time spent with him.

"Well, It's nice seeing you again." I stated embracing him.

"Anytime," he responded. "Hopefully I have another chance to swing by to spend a little more time with you."

"Some other time."

"Alright. You have a safe journey. You hear me."

CHAPTER SIX

While James came from the restroom drying his hands he had seen Gunplay enter inside of the bar. He could tell by his face expression that he was up to something.
As he crossed over the streets Penhead, one of his comrades, had approached him.

"Where are you off to in such a hurry?" Penhead asked.

"To keep an eye out on Gunplay." James said.

"Where is he?"

"I just spotted him walking inside of the bar."

When James and Penhead had walked through the doors he didn't see Gunplay anywhere in sight. James broke the silence.

"Where in the hell is he?" James mumbled.

"He's probably in the back." Penhead mentioned. "You stay here while I go check it out. Just in case he comes out your way."

James leaned against the bar curious to know what Gunplay and his brothers had up their sleeves. Mr. Nelson knocked on the counter and captured his attention.

"Did Old Yellow come by here earlier today?" Mr. Nelson said.

"Mr. Pickett had informed me about it." James stated.

"The way he was looking I could tell that he was up to something."

The sound of chairs breaking had alerted him. It was Gunplay tussling with someone.

"You picked the wrong one buddy" Gunplay spat. He struck the man again with a punch in the face before carrying him out into the streets.

James hurried over before the crowd became too crowded. He pushed Gunplay away as he had challenged the man into a showdown.

"Come on James. Let the man fix his own britches" Gunplay stated.

"Not today." James nodded. "Maybe some other time."

James watched Gunplay spit towards the man's boots before walking away. It only meant one thing, hard time was coming his way.

CHAPTER SEVEN

As I unloaded boxes of peaches from the truck Mr. McElroy came over to join me.

"How's your mother been doing?" Mr. McElroy asked.

"She has been hanging in there I suppose" I replied.

"Have you heard what's been going on in Mount Rush?"

"Haven't heard anything yet."

While I stacked the boxes neatly inside of the corner Mr. McElroy shared with me how the Buchannon boys had been coming to town causing calls.

"Those boys been starting up a bunch of mess since I had splenders inside of my pants." Mr. McElroy said.

"James is a pretty good handyman." I responded. "He'll give them a good fixing if things was to get too out of control."

Mr. McElroy shook his head in a noward motion.

"I don't think so. Not with Michaels boy trailing his tail"

"Who's that?"

"The troublemaker of the West. One of the fastest gunslingers that I have possibly seen that has come storming through that town."

"Hopefully there not up to nothing." I said walking towards the door. "Hopefully it's just another rumor that has spread like wildfire."

Mr. McElroy stopped me in my tracks, handing me a necklace.

"That's for Sherly." he stated. "I think that would probably come in handy to her."

CHAPTER EIGHT

The sweat hit Gunplays open cut as he dugged deep into the hard rock.

"I feel as if James boys are going to be a little problem on our hands." Gunplay stated.

"What makes you think that?" Gunslanger asked.

"The way he was looking the other day when I went to town. The look on his face had takened my appetite."

Gunslanger grab his canteen taking a sip of water. He poured some of it over his neck and wrist to keep cool.

"Let's not put all our attention on him." Gunslanger said. "Let's stay focused on what we have come to do. If he crosses our path, there's nothing that a silver bullet can't handle."

The loud thump underneath Gunpowder shovel alerted him. He continued to strike the ground causing it to sound off.

"I may have found something." Gunpowder mentioned.

Gunplay dropped his shovel and stepped over towards him.

"What do you think it might be?" Gunpowder added.

Gunpowder knelt down removing some of the dust with his hand.

"I can't really tell at this point." Gunplay responded.

While Gunplay and his brothers took turns striking the ground Old Yellow stumbled inside.

"Don't get too comfortable inside of here." Old Yellow mentioned placing his pistol back in his hoster. "Those Redskins aren't just going to give up that easy, especially after you've shedded blood of one of their people." he added. He slid down inside of the hole to join them. "What do you have there?"

"I'm not sure. It's something blocking the way." Gunplay stated.

"Let me take a whack at it," Old Yellow said.

Silence filled the cave as Old Yellow applied pressure towards the earth crust. Old Yellow broke the silence.

"I overheard James and his boys talking earlier when I had gone to town," Old Yellow said.

"About what?" Gunplay asked.

"It wasn't too good. He had our name wrapped up in his conversation." Old Yellow added. "That boy a' starting to get underneath my skin."

Gunpowder rubbed the snot from his nose.

"Maybe we could try to lay low for a few days." Gunpowder mentioned. "I could sense a storm a' coming our way"

Old Yellow nodded his head no.

"If we want to meet our deadline we better keep moving."

CHAPTER NINE

After I had finished making my rounds for that evening Mrs. Rockmore had come over.

"Did you hear about that bank robbery?" Mrs. Rockmore asked.

"Which bank?" I replied.

"The one in Water Valley"

I paused in deep thought. I never knew that Water Valley had a bank due to their population being so small."

Water Valley was a small city. Not too far from the ranch my uncle was raised. It was so small that you could count every single person blind folded while they traveled throughout the town.

"Are you sure it's not Charleston instead of Water Valley?" I asked.

"You calling me a liar?" Mrs. Rockmore placed her hands on her hip.

"Kissing Kate you've better start keeping their ears clear." Mrs. Rockmore slammed her hands on top of the table while leaning closer towards me. "Them Buchannon boys also were spotted with Old Yellow." she added. She wiggled her finger. "I don't like the sound of that Kate. It won't be long before them boys come storming through here."

"Let's not think like that."

"It's better to look for the worst before trouble be a' coming our way"
I shook my head in a noward motion. I knew that I couldn't out argue a woman that had seen twice my years of living. It wasn't any use. I opened the cabinet removing a few bottles of pear preserve so I could give Sherly something to eat before she made it back from a long day of riding.
Mrs. Rockmore broke the silence.

"Don't say I didn't warn you," Mrs. Rockmore said. "I could sense trouble a mile away."

CHAPTER TEN

When James had come back from town the town pioneers were walking throughout the town handing out flyers and small treats out to the townspeople. Penhead approached him from behind as he climbed down off of his horse.

"Have you heard the news?" Penhead asked.

James nodded his head yes.

"I'm thinking that it was those Buchannon Boys" Penhead added. "Mrs. Pickett mentioned to me yesterday that he had seen them track at a high pace as if they were up to something."

"I went by there. The horses that the people had described don't match any of theirs."

"What if they changed horses? Or perhaps them horses were stolen?"

"Lets not think irrational. We can't bring false charges on anyone. It's against the town's law."

While James and Penhead watched the towns mens run towards the pioneers trying to get their share before they had departed, Old Yellow and Gunplay came galloping through.

Penhead broke the silence.

"Where do you think they're headed?" Penhead asked.

"There's no telling with those guys." James responded.

"Maybe we oughta follow them and keep an eye out on them. See what they are stirring up."

James sighed. He picked up a small paper that had blown towards his feet. It was an old paper from the town's cook off. He bawled the paper up, throwing it into the bucket that stood next to the light pole.

"Leave them alone." James said. "Sooner or later things are going to be much clearer that a blind man could see." he added. He walked inside of the bar staring at the two men challenging each other to a quarrel. "Until then, let's continue to tilt our hats and keep our eyes open."

CHAPTER ELEVEN

As James ran water across his face he began to ponder.

"The wind blew hard. The night had settled. There wasn't a star in sight. The buffalos were grazing through the land. I was awakened by someone covering up my mouth.

"SHHH" Injil whispered.

I stared at the Indian woman who had a indian beaded necklace along with a bracelet to match.

"Whats going on?" James whispered.

"My people are coming towards the land."

I was puzzled.

"They are planning on killing the members of your tribe." she added. "You must get going."

As I tied my holster around my neck a brave indian tried to attack me with his spear. I quickly removed my revolver, taking the soul away from him.
The sound of Indians howling in the night had alerted me. I stared at Injil knowing that once they had found her here amongst my people they would surely scalp her.
An arrow filled with flames landed next to my feet almost burning my britches. Some more of them landed out in the land causing the buffalos to scatter. I mounted my horse grasping her by the hand pulling her aboard. As I started to turn my horses around several of indians had circled around me with sticks and axes.

Mr. PIckett approach startled him.

"I didn't mean to scare ya" Mr. Pickett stated.

"It's alright," James replied. He could tell by Mr. PIcketts face expressed that something was terribly wrong. "Is everything alright?"

'I was coming from Water Valley and those Buchanon boys and Old Yellow came storming up a mess in the town. And-"

*James motioned his hands towards him.
"Slow down." James said. "Now, what happened?"*

"Them boys came through town reckoning things" Mr. Pickett stated. "They demanded us to give them what they had wanted as if it was a town of their own." he added. "Penhead tried to stop him but those boys were too much for just one Sherriff."

"Is he alright."

"Of course." Mr.Pickett nodded. "A few men were killed and bruised pretty badly."

James' nose flared up as he hopped on his horse galloping towards the town.

Shortly after he had arrived he immediately noticed that the altercation had elevated from the gunshop. He quickly mounted off of his horse ruching inside.

"James" Leon shouted. "Them boys came through making some fuss."

"What exactly happened?" James asked.

"Them boys came through here high tailing up a storm." Leon added. "They took a few crates of gunpowder."

James was puzzled. What could they possibly have with all of that gunpowder? A western smith didn't use but five to six rounds at the most he thought.

"Where's Penhead?" James asked.

"He went after them." Leon responded. "I tried to stop them but it wasn't much that I could do."

James sighed.

"Tend to the others." he stated. He grabbed an extra case of bullets storming towards the door.

"I should be back shortly. Keep an out on the others."

CHAPTER TWELVE

When I had made it to Mrs. Rockmore's house she was waiting for my arrival.

"What did I tell ya Kate?" Mrs. Rockmore stated. "Them boys came through town just as I had told you."

"They went to that town like a wrecking ball on new year's day." Mrs. Rockmore added. "They are wanted for murder now."

Mrs. Rockmore's last remark had domed in on me. Who did they murder? Was James alright I thought.

"Where did you hear this from?" I asked.

"You know Leon tells me everything" Mrs. Rockmore responded. "He doesn't miss anything like a wide eyed joe buck."

Mrs. Rockmore walked towards the kitchen removing her apron.

"Kate I'm warning you." Mrs Rockmore added. "If those boys dont be brought to a stop there's more than just a small time talk going to occur.

Later that evening when I had arrived home I noticed a letter sticking out of the door. I was curious to know where the letter had come from. Many people that I had associated with never wrote they just simply called.
I opened the letter and began to read:

Dear Kate,

I'm having a small problem with the Buchanon Boys and Old Yellow. They had ambushed the town the other day taking several crates of gunpowder. They also destroyed the town. By tearing the hinges off the door and busting the windows. Did some people get injured? Yes. Some where bruised pretty badly and some were killed. Even my former partner Penhead.
I'm writing to you on the behalf of seeking your help to solve the problem.

Thanks your friend

James

I sighed deeply. Everything that Mrs. Rockmore had been telling me was the truth. I placed the letter on the dresser before heading out the door.

CHAPTER THIRTEEN

As Gunplay had filled his canteen the horse heavily breathing had captured his attention. It was Mr. Pickett.
Mr.Pickett propped his hand on his saddle while chewing his tobacco.

"You mighta as well come clean Gunplay." Mr. Pickett stated.

"What are you talking about?" Gunplay asked.
Mr. Pickett squinted his eyes.

"I know you were the one behind that bank robbery." Mr. Pickett added. "And I know you were behind Penhead's death."

"What?" Gunplay frowned. "You're trying to bring false charges on me and slanders my name."

"I'm not bringing false charges on you. I know that you and your brothers along with Old Yellow have a lot to do with all of this chaos that's been going on around here."

Gunplay sucked his teeth.

"You're challenging me to a draw down." Gunplay asked. He stared at Mr. Pickett tried to read his demeanor to see if he had any illness in him.

"I don't mind giving you a challenge. My guns are ready to smoke any man that stumbles in my path."

"No. I'm not challenging you." Mr. Pickett nodded. "I just want you to know that I know. What you and your boys have going on." he added turning his horse around. "Just know that whatever it is. It didn't last long."

CHAPTER FOURTEEN

The sun was blazing. You could see the heat waves bouncing across the plains. I opened my canteen sprinkling water across my wrist and neck due to the minor heat flashes. The humidity had never been this dry before, at least not while I was traveling.
I began to think about what the Buchanon boys and Old Yellow had up their sleeves. What could they possibly be doing with all that gunpowder I thought.

When people use that much gunpowder they are about to cause a desert storm. But where could they be hiding?
As she drew closer she could spot a few travellers approaching her. Due to the heat and their distance. The cattle that they were hauling had approached me as if they were small dogs. I squinted my eyes trying to make out their images. I knew that if they were wearing casual clothes they were owners of the stock. But if they were cowboys they were workers. Jake tilted his hat towards her approach.

"What a fine young lady like you doing out here traveling by your lonesome?" he asked. "Where are you headed?"

I stared at the rotten teeth that he had disgusted. He seemed to have been chewing on cactus roots his entire life. I really wasn't in the mood to be bothered with him. But never know when you're going to need a favor in return.
I sighed.
"Im headed to Mount Rush." I replied.

"We've just passed through that town," he mentioned. "It seems like they have some trouble on their hands."

"I hope it's not too bad," I stated. I stared at the other men who were passing along. I knew what was going on in Mount Rush. But neither did I want to tell him why I was traveling there, because it was bad.

Especially for the person who was looking similar to a regular one."You might want to take this along with you on your journey."

I was puzzled.

"What for?" I asked.

"There's some Redheads lurking around in the area up ahead." he stated while raising his brow.

"Well, I don't want to hold you up ma'am. I need to get going if I want to reach my destination in time."

CHAPTER FIFTEEN

A few men and women walked throughout the streets still carrying on a conversation about what happened with the Buchanon boys.
James sat out front cleaning his horse hoofs.

"What are you planning to do about those Buchanon Boys?" Leon asked.

James continued to remove the extra layer from the hoofs. He didn't want the town to know that he had sent words to Kate asking for her assistance. He knew if word had gotten out, the town would have an uproarious dispute about what was about to happen and what was going to happen.
James tossed the piece of decay into the tin can.

'I'm not sure." James replied.

"If you need any help my revolver can always stop some people in their tracks." Leon mentioned adjusting himself. "That never had seemed to be a problem to me."

"Thanks, but I'll be fine."

"What are you going to do? You can't take them boys on your own James. Them Buchanon boys are a problem all by themselves. Than with Micheals son traveling their tail youre going to need more than just six chambers."

James sighed deeply. He knew that Leon was right and he probably would need some more gunsman even with Kissing Kate.
After not getting a response out of James Leon broke the silence.

"I could probably send a few words to Danny and his boys if you want."

"Give me some time to think about it." I stated. "If I need any help. I would let you know."

CHAPTER SIXTEEN

Wolff.Wolff.

The night had settled and the coyotes were howling. I laid on the ground with my hat covering my face. As I thought about what trouble lies in front of me I listened to Mr.Flake grazed throughout the land.
A few minutes had passed and I had fallen asleep without noticing it. Mr. Flakes loud cries caused me to awake in a sudden. I looked in his direction noticing that it was a few wild dogs that had stumbled into the area.
I quickly aroused from my resting point grabbing a tree branch trying to run them off the more it seemed like more had appeared.
Mr. Flake reared up and began to sprint into the night.
The wild dogs howls hoovering in the night from each angle had my heels clicking.
It wasn't long before a few Redskins came in to help. I was overwhelmed due to their good spirit because I had left my pistol strapped to my saddle. But it began to dome in on me that I was traveling alone, which wasn't very good to a pack of Redskins scalp laying next to their body.
The young brave stepped towards. He couldn't be no more than twelve years of age.

"Thanks." I stated extending my hand out.

The brave ignored my greeting.

"What brings you through heading to Mount Rush." I added. I looked at the other braves who were creeping up as if the prey that they were hunting. "I wasn't looking to cause any problems."

The brave motioned his hands at a few of his members. As they embraced my hands together. I only had one thing on my mind. *Would I make it out alive in time*.

CHAPTER SEVENTEEN

The sun hadn't quite risen over the horizon. Gunplay and his brothers were off to an early start. Gunplay removed the sweat with his handkerchief.

"We must move double time." Gunplay mentioned. "That Pickett boy has been hitchhiking my trail." "We can't move any faster than our two hands could fix a horse bridle." Gunslanger stated.

Gunplay nodded his head in disagreement.

"Old Yellow haven't been helping out much at all around here." Gunslanger added. "I don't see why we're even carrying him along with us."

"Yeah, I think he's just trying to hitch a free ride." Gunpowder mentioned. "And I'm not going for that."

Gunplay grinded his teeth.

"Lets not speak such harsh words." Gunplay spat. "He has done just as much work as I have."

Old Yellow belt clicking had captured their attention.

"I just got news that Danny and his boys are coming to town." Old Yellow said.

Old Yellow glanced at each of them seeing that they were talking behind his back. One of the things that he did not accept. He thought about smoking them, but there was too much money laying out in front of him.

"What for?" Gunpowder repeated.

"I'm not sure. But you know that they probably would be eager to help that ole' ranger out with tracking us down."

"Danny isn't much of a problem. But his boys may be. I never-"

"Any man is a problem to me that could be the death of me." Old Yellow stated.

Gunplay remained silent. He never thought that he would ever hear those words depart the lips of one of the quickest gunslangers in the west. Was Old Yellow scared? Was he trying to belittle himself and make people think less of him? Or was he trying to see where our heart set with him I thought.

Gunplay shook the thought away.

"I agree with you there Old Yellow." Gunplay said. "Danny isn't someone to look over. He could gun down just as fast as Peter Gunz. And he's quite handy with his holsters."

Gunpowder and Gunslanger looked at each other. Were their brothers sniffing another man ass they thought.

"From now on we travel in pairs." Old Yellow stated. "Just in case things may get a little smoke inside." Gunplay continued to slam his axe inside of the dirt. He refused to let any pioneer or deputy ruin his plans that he had worked so hard to plan.

CHAPTER EIGHTEEN

After I had left Chief Acxing and his tribe it wasn't long before I had made it to Mount Rush. The place had changed in its entirety since the last time that I had visited. The townhouses as well as their departments had changed from pinewood to gopher wood. They had opened up a shoemaker store and the small bar that I had two corridor doors rather than the old copper door.
James came out of Leon's workshop smiling from ear to ear. It had been a minute since I had seen him. His facial hair had filled in making him look as if he was wolverine. His shoulders had expanded and his chest stuck out as if he had on an iron plate.

"Kissing Kate!" James continued to smile. "It's been awhile. I thought at first you didn't remember me."

"I would have been here twice as fast. But I stormed into some trouble up ahead."

"What happened?"

"I stumbled across some redskins."

"Redskins?" James stated. "Which way did you take?"

"Across El Valle."

James nodded his head. Most indians that had found a westerner traveling alone wouldn't have allowed you to see another day. Kate and she were beautiful. Her long golden goldilocks were stuffed under her hat and the pony tail that she wore feld down to her lower back. Her eyes were brown and her wide gorgeous smile that she exposed had cowboys boots running laps around the place.

"Mr. Flake and I were ambushed by some wild dogs." I chuckled.

"If it wasn't for the braves I wouldn't be here with you."

Mr. Pickett approaching them at a fast pace had captured their attention.

"What seems to be the problem?" James asked.

"I've spotted Gunplay and his brothers out by that cave." he mentioned.

"What cave."

"The one over yonder by the creek were the Buffalo blows."

"There's no telling." Mr. Pickett stated. "I tried to get closer up on them to see what it was that they were doing," he added. "But Old Yellow had started to approach from the other wing."

James and I adjusted ourselves while Mr. Pickett tried to keep his horse steady.

"That's when I knocked it into high gear. Getting the hell out of there."

"I'm not sure. If they did , it wasn't nothing but my inner spirit left standing there waving them goodbye."

I became curious. The only thing that could possibly be going on at a cave was goldmine. But I knew that it had never been gold found in this area, especially Mount Rush.

CHAPTER NINETEEN

As Gunplay had tied the bags of beef jerky to carry back to the cave for his brothers to eat, Old Yellow had come riding up the hill to his place.

"Did you hear about that gal?" Gunplay asked.

"What gal?" Old Yellow replied.

"Kissing Kate."

"What's she doing here?"

"She's here to help that sheriff boy."

Old Yellow knew that he had hell on his wheels. Kissing Kate was one of the fastest female gunslanger that sent a bullet flying at you before the sound of the clock had sounded ding dong. Not only that she was a woman. A woman that outdrew most men that didn't deserve the stripes thaat were wearing.

"Did she bring any travelers?" Old Yellow asked.

"She was spotted riding in by herself." Gunplay stated. "What do you think we ought to do?"

"Let's continue to dig until tomorrow and see what tomorrow brings."

CHAPTER TWENTY

It thundered and lightning but there still wasn't any sign of rain. James. Danny and I were sitting over by the pine trees watching the cave.

"What do you expect that they are up to." Danny asked.

"I'm not sure." James replied.

"They're probably digging that for sure."

"Digging for what though."

"There must be a goldmine inside of there."

"But there isn't any gold found around here."

I watched Gunplay and Old Yellow standing at the front entrance holding a conversation. Neither of them seemed to be paying us any attention. I could tell by their clothes that they were digging that for sure.

I broke the silence. "Do you think they could be digging a tunnel." I suggested.

"Digging that's for sure. But where about I don't know." James stated.

"Maybe we should check up on the place. See what we could find." Danny mentioned.

I sighed.

“That's a waste of time.” James added. “I've been traveling around this place since I was a little boy.” he added. “I know every back hill and rabbit hole around here.”

Danny grinned.

“Then what do you want to do?” Danny asked. “By us debating isn't going to get the problem done.”

“I know. But we must be patience. We don't want to blow our cover.'

CHAPTER TWENTY ONE

Gunplay spit on the ground as him and Old Yellow rode towards the cave.

“I had spotted some fresh tracks over yonder.” Gunplay pointed. “I think that Mr. Pickett boy has been watching us come to and from this cave.”

“He could watch us all he wants.” Old Yellow replied. “There's nothing he nor that gal could do to stop us.”

As they climbed the hill approaching the cave entrance. Gunpowder and Gunslanger had met him.

"We're just about done," Gunpowder mentioned. "It won't be long before the other side come a' caving in."

"That'll be on time. Because we need all the lead we could get. Especially with those rangers our ass."

"Speaking of them." Gunslanger said. "I saw him and that gal up stream. As if they were trying to sniff out our trails."

Gunplay sighed.

"It won't be long before they come raging inside of here." Gunpowder stated.

"We'll be long gone before they decide to come." Old Yellow replied. "If not my guns dont mind handling any problems for me."

Gunplay propped his feet on top of the rock in deep thought. He pictured each scenario on how things would play out. The good as well as the bad.
He shook the thoughts away realizing that regardless of however it was going to play out he was going to make a way out for his brothers. Because he was wanted for murder.

CHAPTER TWENTY TWO

I had awakened early that morning to go keep an eye out on things on my own. Without it being any gold

being found here and a stream blocking off the back
entrance I couldn't manage to think where they could
be digging too.
The snapping of the twigs and the heavy breathing
from horses nostrils had startled me. I reached for my
snug nose looking to draw down until I had noticed
that it was James approaching me.

"I kind of figured that you would be here since I didn't
see your horse tied down outside." James said.
"Have you spotted any sign of them."

"Not at this moment." I nodded. "Everything had been
completely quiet around here except the crickets
chipping and the wind blowing."

As James and I sat there discussing on what they
could possibly be up to. Gunpowder and Gunslanger
had came riding in with a few more horses.

"What do they need with horses." I mumbled.

"I'm not sure" he replied.

"That's there get away." Danny joined them.
"Whenever the horses run hot." he added. "They're
probably going to be traveling far."

"But where."

"I'm not sure."

I paused in deep thought contemplating for a moment before breaking the silence.

"Do you think they could be headed to Long Horn." I asked.

"That's too far." James replied. "Besides there's a sheer drop inside of the canyon heading west of here."

"Do you think they could be headed east." I mentioned. "There is a narrow crossing there."

"Nah"

"What about Charleston."

"But what's in Charleston that they could possibly want."

"Cattle." Danny added. "I heard that it's a large trade mark there."

"I don't think that they would be digging a hole. Just to bring some cattle back."

"Than what do you think."

I sighed as silence stood between us.

"There's no telling." I stated "But I betcha that's where they headed."

CHAPTER TWENTY THREE

The rooster crowed and the crickets continued to chirp in a rhythm. The town was still asleep except for the deputies and his boys.
As Gunplay crept through the streets the cool breeze hit his face. He hid behind the nicely stacked crates glancing throughout the streets for any signs of awareness. He watched the light on the grocery store continuing to blink on and off before he started to make another move.
While he veered around the corner he stumbled across of the deputies.

"What are you doing back here stalking the streets as if you're some type of their in the night." Johnny stated.

Gunplay chuckled.

""My name isn't Peter Swift if I ever touch something that doesn't belong to me." Gunplay said.

"Well, you need to get where you are headed. We don't want to mistaken you for a disaster that happens. Than you end up tied down to a cow stake underneath the blazing sun all day."

Gunplay simply tilted his hat and walked across the streets. He didn't bother to look back because he knew that the deputy was probably still watching him.

When he had caught up with the others to the bank the bankrolled was arriving.

"We might want to be careful." Gunplay whispered. "Those deputies are stalking the streets."

"They want be a problem." Old Yellow replied.

"How's things looking"

"Only pleasant enough for the eyes to see."

The clicking of slings and rolling tires captured our attention. Gunplay watched the husky man ride through the streets slowly.

"Where could he be headed." Gunplay asked.

"Probably just passing through." Old Yellow stated. "There's not much that he could do unless he going towards the bank."

As the last word rolled off of Old Yellow tongue the man pulled in front of the bank.

"Seem as if we pick the right time." Gunpowder mentioned.

"What do you mean" Old Yellow said.

"That's the money truck."

"I really wasn't expecting for this to happen."

Old Yellow smiled from ear to ear.

"Yeah." he nodded. "That only means one thing."

"What?" Gunslangers asked.

"There's plenty more of it to add to the pile."

"I love the sound of that." Gunplay stated.

After they had unloaded the wagon Gunplay removed his pistol is allowing them to lead the way.

"Didn't mean to disturb you boys." Gunplay stated.

The husky man reached for his pistol. Before you knew it Old Yellow had drawn down.

BOOM BOOM
BOOM BOOM

As Gunplay grabbed the last money bag exiting out of the door the deputies and his boys were hurrying over.

BOOM BOOM
BOOM BOOM

"Got damn it" Johnny spat through clenched teeth. "One thing that I hate on this mother login earth is a theft in the night."

BOOM BOOM

Gunplay fired a few rounds towards them as he mounted on his horse. He kicked his horse in high gear galloping away into the night.

CHAPTER TWENTY FOUR

While I tried my saddle down in place James and Danny were approaching me.

"Good morning" I said. "It's a fine morning to go bull riding."

James chuckled. It had been awhile since the last time that he had came face to face with a bull. The last time he had tipped one the bull had carried him on a helluva ride. It wasn't for Injil awakening up in the middle of the night he would probably be either dead or still running.

"I was thinking maybe we could swing around by the creek. Therefore we could get a much better veiw." I added.

"I don't see any problem with that." James said. He mounted on his horse as Danny come over to join us. "As long as we bring him down into a fox hole."

As we rode towards the cave Danny had shared with us a story into the morning. The sound of horses echoed through The cave alerting us. It wasn't long before we brought the in a more better view. The Buchannon Boys and Old Yellow came a galloping out of the entrance at a fast pace.
I broke the silence that stood in our presence.

"Just like I had expected." I stated. "Bank robbers."

"It had been awhile since I ripped off anything."

Gunplay looked over his shoulders spotting us coming towards them.

"There goes them boys and that gal." Gunplay shouted.

"I'm sick of these bastards." Gunslanger stated through clenched teeth."I've been had enough of him." he added. "I'm about to put his ass away for good, that's for sure."

Gunshots were fired and final one had filled the air. I shouted at the top of my lungs at Mr. Flake to kick it in high gear.

BOOM. BOOM.
BOOM. BOOM.

I locked eyes on Gunplay as Danny roped
Gunpowder off before snatching him off of his horse.
I refused to be apart of a rodeo that my cow picker
got away.

BOOM. BOOM.

As Mr. Flake and I went down the hill after Gunplay
we began to slide. It had surprised me to see that Mr.
Flake had remained calm. Normally he would be
started and act of control.

BOOM. BOOM.

My hat came flying off of my head after Gunplay fired
a few rounds at me.
I removed my rope winding it up in mid air before
throwing it. I snatched him from his saddle and onto
the ground.
As I mounted off of my horse heading towards him he
removed the rope gaining control of his feet.

BOOM.BOOM.
BOOM.BOOM

Gunplay cried out.

"Don't worry Kissing Kate." Gunplay shouted
breathless. "I'll see you in hell."

"I can't wait." I replied.

I place my pistol back into my holster turning my attention towards James and Danny. They waved there hat in mid air informing that they had broke the bull down without much words left to say.

www.ingramcontent.com/pod-product-compliance
Lightning Source LLC
Chambersburg PA
CBHW021403160726
47994CB00007B/3054